How Many Days to my Birthday?

First U.S. Edition   1   2   3   4   5   6   7   8   9   10

Library of Congress Cataloging in Publication data was not available in time for publication of this
book, but can be obtained from the Library of Congress.
ISBN 0-688-11236-6   ISBN 0-688-11237-4 (lib. bdg.)
L.C. Number 91-53022

How Many Days
to my Birthday?

Gus Clarke

Lothrop, Lee & Shepard Books
New York

"It's not fair," said Danny. "Everyone has birthdays except me."

It seemed like years since he'd had one of his own.

They said Florence-Next-Door had already had *six*!

And even the cat had had more than him.

"So why can't *I* have a birthday?" he wanted to know.

Mom said let go and he could. She hadn't forgotten. It wouldn't
be long.

But it seemed like a long time to Danny.

"How many days to my birthday?" he would say

now and again.

Mom said it might help if they made up a chart. He could cross off the days. "Yes, please," said Danny...

...and crossed off the days. "But it's *still* not my birthday," he said.

And sometimes he thought it would never come.

But Mom said it would. (And the sooner the better.)

So he sent out a few invitations. Just one or two very close
friends.

And he made up his mind for his present.

Several times.

He made a nice cake.

He blew up the balloons. There was nothing much more he could do.

Except wait... just a little bit longer... until...

"Happy Birthday, Danny!" said Mom.

And it was.

"Well," said Mom. "Was it worth waiting for?"

"Yes, Mom," said Danny. "But, Mom..."

"How many days till Christmas?"